A Tangle of Brungles

Shobha Viswanath | Culpeo S. Fox

A COVEN OF WITCHES
With hair full of gnats,
Lived on a hill
With A CLOWDER OF CATS.

On a full moon night,
Under A GALAXY OF STARS,
A PACK OF WOLVES
Howled from afar.

"I think I will marry,"
Cried the witch with a wart.
"Let's summon Brungle,
The king of my heart!

He is so bad,
So wickedly vile.
I love his grotesque
And dastardly style.

To bring Brungle here,
A broth we must brew.
Go find the black book for

The Great Brungle Stew."

As the witches began
Their terrible broth,
A PARLIAMENT OF OWLS
Flew in from the north.

A WAKE OF BUZZARDS
Gathered for the fun,
While A MURDER OF CROWS
Cawed, one by one.

"A QUIVER OF COBRAS,
Shoot them in straight.
From A LOUNGE OF LIZARDS
Add exactly eight!

Make sure to toss in
A MISCHIEF OF MICE.
Or just one big rat
Is sure to suffice."

"To make it much tangier,
Add two rotten gourds,
A MESS OF IGUANAS
And A KNOT OF BIG TOADS!

For a little bit of color,
A GLINT OF GOLDFISH.
A KALEIDOSCOPE OF BUTTERFLIES
Will complete the dish.

A CLEW OF WORMS
Will serve as garnish,
With A CLUTTER OF SPIDERS
Soaked in varnish."

The witches stirred
Their cauldron of lead,
As A CLOUD OF BATS
Circled overhead.

"Tremple Gemple Fever Sticks
Pimple Poxile Psittacosis
Frungle Brungle, Where Are You?
Appear Now! Shimshamshoo!"

The big black pot
Shivered and shook.
Smoke filled the air
As the brewing broth cooked.

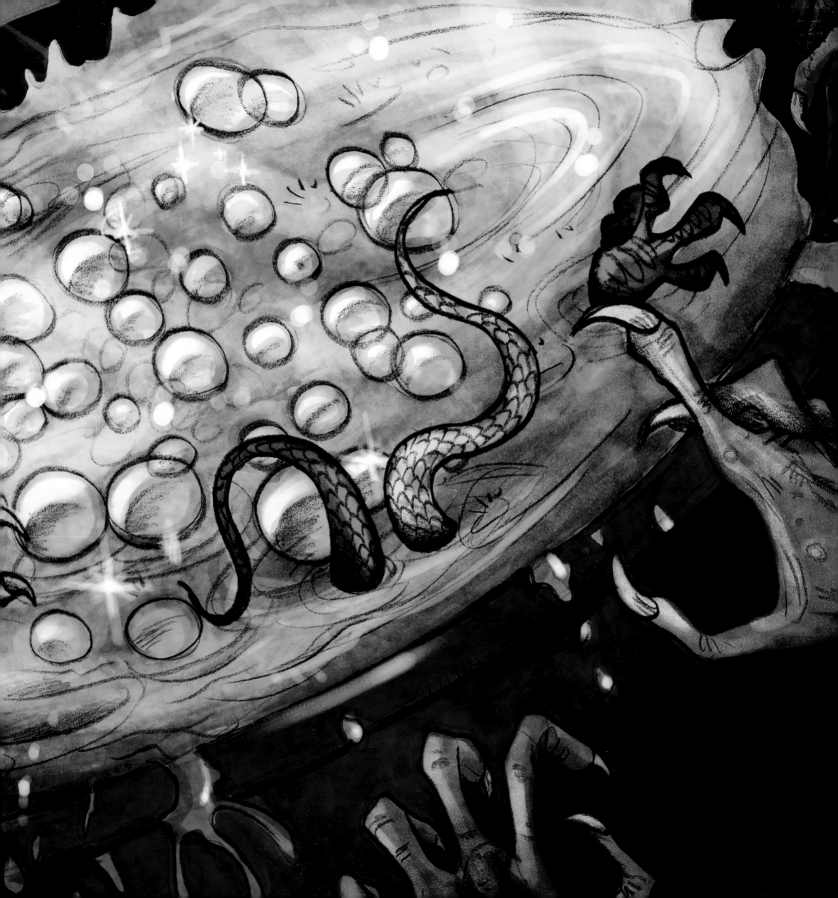

A BEVY OF SWANS
And A BANNER OF KNIGHTS
Came dancing and singing
In bright orange tights.

A MUSTER OF PEACOCKS
And A PADDLE OF DUCKS
Followed a scurrying
FALL OF WOODCHUCKS.

The witches waited
But where was Brungle?
They gasped as they watched
And asked "Did we bungle?"

"Didn't we make the right potion?"
"What on earth went wrong?"
"Did we forget the worms?"
"Did we mess up the song?"

"Quiet!" said the old witch.
"'We'll fix this at midnight.
Just one BIND OF EELS
Will make it all right."

With the slithering eels in,
The bubbling broth roiled.
Soon out of the pot
Something uncoiled.

First came the arms,
Then came the legs,
Then came the antennae,
And twelve Brungle heads.

Twelve tentacles rose.
So did half a dozen tails!
And at each tentacle's end
Were five neon nails!

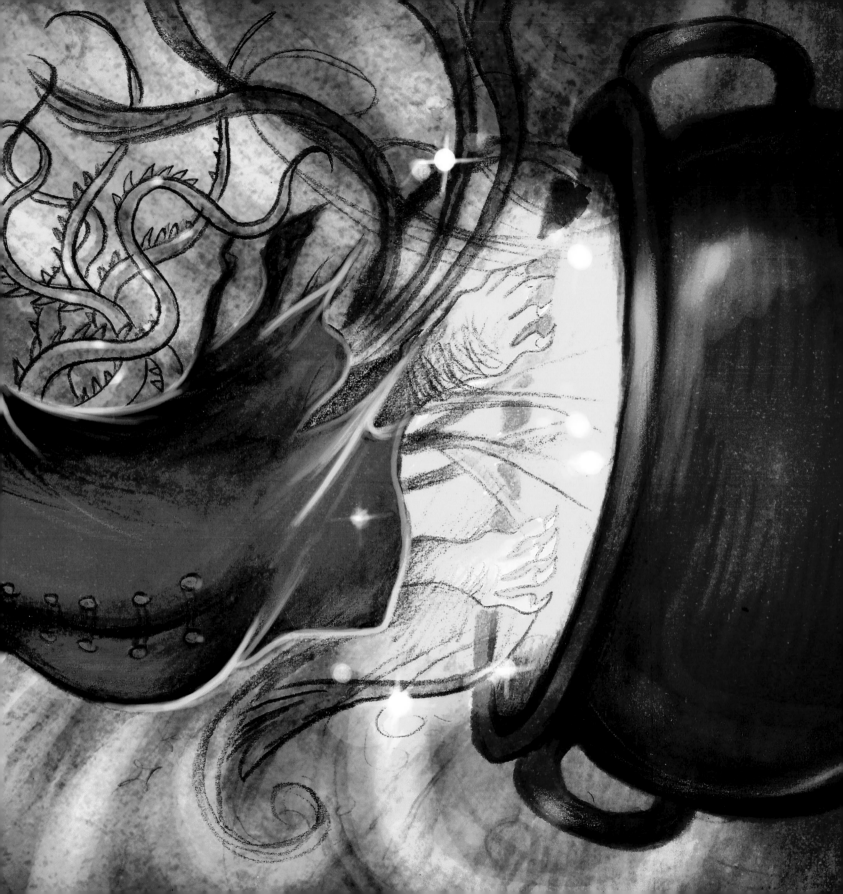

Poor old Brungle
Looked around in shock.
He tripped on his tails
As he tried to walk.

"Ha Ha Ha, Tee Hee Hee,
It is he! It is he!"
The witches cackled
With mirth and with glee.

"A TANGLE OF BRUNGLES
So hideous, so shocking!
A Brungle per witch,
How devilish! How rocking!"

"A Brungle per witch?
Have you lost your mind?
Surely there's an
INCANTATION OF WARLOCKS
you'll find."

So said Brungle
Declining to be wed,
And gathering his tails
He turned around and fled.

Author

SHOBHA VISWANATH is the
co-founder and publishing director
of Karadi Tales Company, and
lives in Chennai.

Illustrator

CULPEO S. FOX is an artist and illustrator with a
bachelor's degree in Graphic Design. Currently living and
working in Germany, Fox is best known for the self-
defining concept of Method Art. Her deep love for wildlife
informs Fox's focus on nature and animal art in her work.

A Tangle of Brungles

© and ℗ 2018 Karadi Tales Company Pvt. Ltd.

Text: Shobha Viswanath
Illustrations: Culpeo S. Fox

Karadi Tales Company Pvt. Ltd.
3A, Dev Regency, 11, First Main Road
Gandhinagar, Adyar, Chennai 600020
Tel: +91 44 4205 4243
email: contact@karaditales.com
Website: www.karaditales.com

ISBN: 978-81-8190-360-0

Printed at: Mentor Printing and Logistics Pvt. Ltd., India

Cataloging - in - Publication information:

Viswanath, Shobha
A Tangle of Brungles / Shobha Viswanath; illustrated by Culpeo S. Fox
p.32; color illustrations; 24.5 x 24 cm.

1. Travel--Juvenile literature. 2. Conduct of life--Humor.
3. Conduct of life--Juvenile fiction. 4. Selfishness--Juvenile fiction.

PZ7   [E]

JUV019000 JUVENILE FICTION / Humorous Stories
JUVENILE FICTION / Social Issues / Manners & Etiquette
JUV068000 JUVENILE FICTION / Travel

ISBN 978-81-8190-360-0

Distributed in the United States by Consortium Book Sales & Distribution
www.cbsd.com